I0741454

WHIPSTICK

STORIES FROM CENTRAL VICTORIA

First published by Accidental Publishing 2018

Cataloguing-in-Publication entry is available from the National Library of Australia
http://catalogue.nla.gov.au

ISBN 978-0-9954425-4-2 (paperback)
Fiction A808.3

Typeset in 9 pt Georgia
Printed and bound by Ingram

Accidental Publishing
An imprint of Of The World Books
PO Box 8070 Bendigo South LPO VIC 3550
Australia

www.oftheworldbooks.com

Accidental Publishing

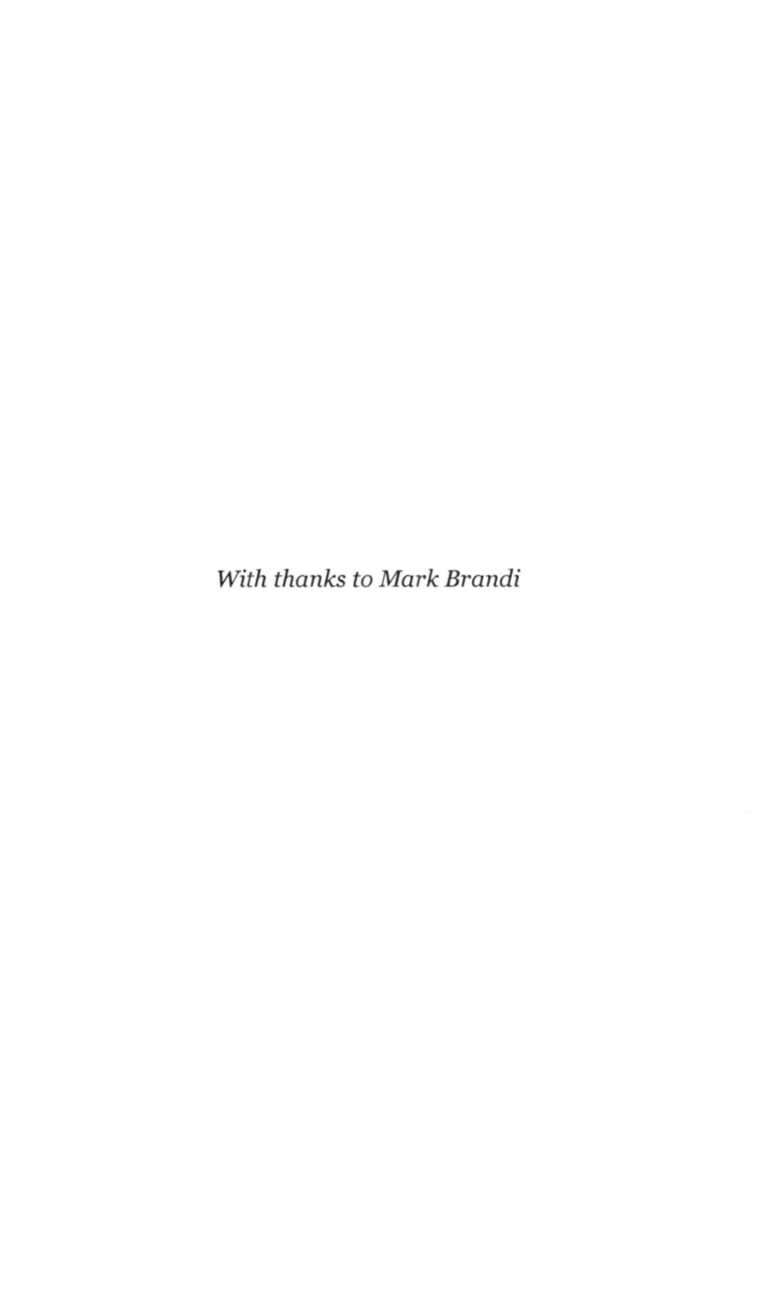

With thanks to Mark Brandi

Where it began...

IN April 2018, five emerging writers gathered in the historic Mechanics Institute building at Eaglehawk for a writing workshop conducted by Mark Brandi, author of the award-winning crime novel, *Wimmera*. Their topic was **Whipstick**, and during the workshop and in the weeks following, they developed stories with Mark's help.

The end result is this small compilation – the first ever story collection to come out of this haunting landscape country north of Bendigo.

We also asked two well-known Bendigo authors to share their own responses to the Whipstick. Lauren Mitchell brings her much-loved brand of whimsy and compassion to the Introduction, and Dianne Dempsey provides our Postscript, an excerpt from her novel, *Girls In Our Town*, which is set in and around Eaglehawk and the Whipstick.

We thank the Regional Centre for Culture for supporting this writing project, Mark Brandi for being such a generous and helpful workshop mentor, the writers who took part, and Amy Doak, publisher extraordinaire, who is a fine example of the expertise to be found in our creative city.

CONTENTS

Welcome to the Whipstick
Lauren Mitchell

LET me take you to the top of Lightning Hill in the Whipstick Forest north of Bendigo. It's midday, early winter, and a grey sky covers a canopy of box-ironbark forest that stretches the whole horizon. It's a trick, this view. You'd have no idea the city beyond was just there below. Or that you could walk south for 20 minutes and be sitting at my kitchen table with a cup of tea and a mint slice biscuit. If you didn't know better, you'd consider yourself well and truly lost. This Whipstick, it's a shape shifter.

Dodder-laurel vines hang from box gums like macabre Christmas tinsel. The caw of distant crows down in Whitehorse Gully echo, long and slow, like the lonely wails of lost children. There are spirits here. Everyone feels them, regardless of belief.

Bendigo writer Dianne Dempsey explores that energy in her novel *Girls in Our Town*. Of this place Dianne's main character Sheba says; "The Whipstick is harsh, sandstone country with little water, covered by a dense mass of box-ironbark, Mallee eucalyptus, wattle and dodder-laurel vines. In the early days of the gold rush, these parasitic vines were so pervasive they created huge webs in which the diggers would often become lost and caught like flies, they suffered desperate, lonely deaths.

"But before the diggers there were the Dja Dja Wurrung people, and before them there were the spirits – ghost creatures – who were disturbed when the miners sunk their shafts and dug their tunnels."

The Whipstick stretches north from Eaglehawk to Raywood and east to Kamarooka. Miners named it after the nature of its foliage and today the forest remains a rare example of its kind. It's believed up to 85 per cent of Australia's box-ironbark forests have been destroyed.

Gold was first discovered here in 1852 and evidence of the flurry to find riches is everywhere. Be careful not to venture far from the haphazard paths, for the understorey hides shafts and shallow diggings not worth risking life and limb for.

I realise I may not be selling this place to you. Certainly it's not really somewhere you'd come for a holiday. There are no resort retreats, no Instagram accounts dedicated to its views, no Trip Advisor reviews. It's not a place that will advance your social standing. You won't brag about it. But that's the point really. The benefits are all internal. The 'Sticks' is a place to check in with yourself. I often come for that very reason.

The forest looms heavy behind the Eaglehawk neighbourhood where I live, a short walk past flat-faced houses and up a rough path between properties. If the sun is angled just so through the black trunks, it's gorgeous.

All but one backyard abutting the bush is blocked out by a continuous stretch of high steel fencing. Only one woman has chosen to face her home open to the forest. I asked her once what it was like to live with it. She said she loves it. She feels its seasons, sees its birds. She thinks it's beautiful.

Those fences are a firm, thin delineator between that place and this. Which is the real world? I think it's the forest and that's also why I'm drawn to it. The Whipstick is the way life's meant to be here. This is ironbark country. It's a place that makes you face your fears, of the unknown and the elements. It awakens ancient instincts. Places like this are rare so close to the business of everyday life. Of meals to cook and clothes to wash, homework to oversee and deadlines to meet. Don't we all want to escape those daily doings from time-to-time and return to the elements we're made of? Don't you?

I interviewed an artist recently, a woman of national significance who 12 months earlier had moved to Eaglehawk at the age of 85. She'd never even heard of the suburb until she came to look at a Victorian house that caught her heart.

She spoke of the towns and cities she'd lived in and of travels throughout central Australia's red heart and to places like Lake Mungo, southern New South Wales, the world's oldest cremation site. Well-thumbed folios of charcoal drawings from past days in the Mungo dust were shelved among walls of books in her living room. Dark drawings of abstract figures, smudged and grainy. They weren't beautiful, not in a traditional sense, and she said: "I used to try to get the energy out of the earth and the energy of the people who lived there would come to me. All those places have it for me. I don't like nice countryside." I replied: "Well, you need to go to the Whipstick." I said she'd be in good company, for this place has long inspired creative souls. This anthology of stories is the perfect example. Here are some more...

When a photographer friend of mine suggested we collaborate on a book about artist spaces of the Victorian goldfields, I agreed on one condition; we track down John Wolseley. It's well known he calls the Whipstick home, and I'd long wanted to meet him. The artist largely divides his time between this forest, his Melbourne studio and Arnhem Land. When we found him he'd recently returned from the top end to his bush bolthole; a studio twice the size of a standard house, a sort of concrete bunker with a sway roof to mimic the months he spends under canvas. It's not exactly warm and welcoming, but its owner is. John ushered us in, placed a blackened kettle on a gas ring, brewed us tea and started talking. I barely asked him a question and simply tried to keep up.

Long story short, John was born in England in 1938. He lived and worked throughout Europe before coming to Australia in 1976. He first came to Bendigo in the 1980s as an artist-in-residence at the local arts college. One of the lecturers lived in the Whipstick, which is how John encountered this place. "I visited Stanley Farley next door, who was teaching there at the time," John said. "He took me on a walk through the forest and I found this place. Stanley said he thought it was for sale, so I bought it. I sort of fell in love with the Whipstick. I realised it's an incredibly unusual, beautiful forest if you know how to look at it." John said not everyone does. "Some call it bush burial country."

Google 'Whipstick history' and you'll find a watercolour, charcoal and pencil work of John's on the National Gallery of Victoria site that demonstrates how he sees this place.

Our next stop for the book was Stanley, who lives a crow's call away from John in a house he and his wife constructed themselves using leftover sandstone from the Cathedral build in Bendigo. The mixed media sculptor works from a former train carriage well bedded down in the bush.

Stan and his wife bought their 20 acre Whipstick block in 1976. "I didn't think we'd stay here," he said. "I just wanted a piece of land and to get out of Melbourne. I like living in the landscape, I always have. I like being in the organic world. That's very important to me."

Stan's early years were spent around family properties to the state's north east, around the Ovens Valley. "It's very different to here and I always had in mind I'd go to the north east," he said. "My idea of the country used to be lushness, thick, soft and green. We came here and it was all black and red and bare.

I didn't like it at all, but I thought it'd do for a time. Turns out it grew on us and after a while we couldn't leave. Now, when I look at lush country I don't like it, I've totally reversed. I see the colours and the details here. I like the extremities of heat and cold and it gets very cold here and very hot."

When we visited it was whip cold. Rain had amplified the colours. Ironbark trunks were coal black. Yellow box streaky white. Hot pink blossoms of flowering gums punctuated the green. Millions of wet mirrored leaves fluttered.

Twelve months after that book was finished I became very unwell. That winter was wasted alternating between my bed and the couch. I spent far too long under doonas. Under artificial heating. There's nothing like the cutting in and out, in and out of a ducted gas system long day after day to make you yearn for boots and a scarf, your dogs by your side and the chill of crisp bush air on your cheeks.

I begged my beloveds to take the walk for me and report back. I was sure the wattle would be flowering and it would be the first season I'd missed it in 14 years here. They returned with a sprig of blooms. Tiny tufts of winter sunshine, gently placed in a blue pottery vase to pepper our kitchen table with pollen. It was better than a dozen roses any day.

•

Ashes and Dust
Wendy Bridges

2016

LISA hadn't expected the train carriage to be still standing and her heart gave a jolt when she saw it through the bush beyond the dam. She'd snuck through the fence to look at what had been her backyard for most of her teenage years.

In her backpack she carried the ashes of her mum and dad. She planned to scatter them in the forest after carrying them from house to house for too many years. Twenty in fact. An accident on this very road in the Whipstick. Their car forced off the road and into a tree by a drunk hoon before he crashed into one himself. Afterwards, Lisa had sold the property and hadn't set foot in the area since.

It was still early. She'd always liked to be in the forest alone in the mornings when the dew still sweetened the air. And the birds. How had she forgotten the birds? At that time of day the magpies ruled – warbling to each other and – Lisa had always imagined – to her. She always talked to the magpies. *If you talk to them, they won't swoop you*, her dad always said. It worked. She'd never been swooped – not once in her fifty-odd years.

She had always felt safest in the forest in the mornings, when no one else was about. Later in the day prospectors, picnickers and walkers could pop up anywhere. And at night – well that was another story altogether. From dusk, as the birds quietened and the cicadas took their place in the forest soundtrack, the place became eerie and threatening. She remembered the heart-in-mouth moments as cars revved on the road at the front of their block. The skin prickles and pounding pulse as a carload of guys in their hotted-up Holden chucked VB cans out the window and let rip with wolf-whistles and howls when they saw her walking along the driveway. She shuddered at the memory – fourteen-year-old girls alone in the bush didn't usually fare well with a carload of drunk youths.

Her parents had bought the block of land carved out of the Whipstick, and while her dad built their house they had lived in that wooden train carriage. It was old and creaky then, but now, although still technically standing, it had become dilapidated and looked to have been abandoned entirely by the current owners.

She pulled open the door and stepped inside. Her eyes took a few moments to adjust. The old shelves her dad had banged together for her books were the only thing that suggested past habitation. And face down, shoved at the back of the top shelf, was an old book – *The Little Prince.*

She wiped the decades of brown dust off the cover and flipped through its pages.

1979

Lisa heard the crunch of footsteps and spun around whip-fast, her skin prickling. She scrambled to her feet as a guy approached with his hands up apologetically in front of him.

"Sorry – sorry," he said. "I didn't mean to scare you."

She looked at him, avoiding eye-contact, and brushed the dirt from her jeans. Her grasp of language seemed to have abandoned her. He stood before her, tall and gangly with bushy dark hair and a baggy green t-shirt.

"I don't bite." He grinned. "I'm David. You live on the block over there don't you?" He pointed back to her place.

And although it wasn't visible, Lisa knew it was close enough that a sprint would have her back there if things got weird.

"I...yeah." Lisa brushed her hair out of her eyes and made herself look at him. He must have seen her before. Her insides fluttered.

"My parents have the farm over the road," he said. "I guess we're neighbours. Hi there neighbour!"

"Hi." She couldn't help laughing at his goofy grin.

They sat and chatted for what seemed like ages. Or more accurately David chatted and Lisa muttered a reply every now and then to his questions. By the time he walked her back to the fence behind her place, she felt sure they were going to be friends.

"See ya round," David turned and wandered off back along the path. And as she clambered back through the fence Lisa thought that maybe the loneliness she felt, stuck with just her parents in the middle of the bush might be about to diminish.

Lisa made a point of walking around the perimeter of the block, down along the road and back, every day since she had met David in the hope he would appear again. But there had been no sign.

After a week of scorching, skin-blistering weather, one afternoon it was almost dark by 4.30. The clouds had come in on the wind before everything went still and the air felt heavy. Then wham. The rain came pelting down while Mum was cooking dinner on the old slow combustion stove that stood between the train carriage and the campfire. The stove had come with them when they moved from the Dandenongs. Lisa watched her through the window standing out there in a raincoat, the rain spitting and steaming as it landed on the stove. Dad was shoving more wood in the box to keep the fire alight long enough to finish cooking dinner.

Lisa had been trying to read in the fading light. She lit some candles before abandoning the idea to stand and watch as the water rose, forming a shallow but rapid river around the train carriage.

The campfire was all but out and the amount of rain going down the stove's flue meant that the dinner was as ready as it ever would be. Lisa opened the door for Mum and the food. Dad followed with the gas lamp, its normally loud hissing all but drowned out by the rain hammering the roof. The windows fogged up quickly as the space filled with their breath, and discarded raincoats hung from hooks by the door. At times like this the carriage felt smaller than ever.

After dinner Lisa made an origami boat and set it to sail out the door. She scrawled a secret message on it and imagined it sailing down the drive-way river and across the road to David's door.

The next morning the forest glistened as the sun shone on the raindrops that clung to the trees and the puddles that lay across the block. Lisa was getting some dry wood from under the tarp behind the train carriage while Dad swept out the campfire that was clogged with muddy dregs from the night before.

"Hi there neighbour," said a familiar voice and Lisa almost dropped the wood on her feet. She turned to see David extending his hand to her dad and introducing himself.

"Mum thought I should come and check that you weren't completely flooded out after the rain."

"Very good of you," said Dad, "We're fine. The carriage held up well – not a drop inside."

"Lisa, come and meet our neighbour, David," Dad took the wood from her and set it in the fire pit.

"Good to meet you Lisa," David said.

Lisa was relieved. She hadn't told her parents about their chance meeting in the bush.

"Go and get your mum, love, and bring out another mug. David, you'll stay for a cup of tea? The billy's nearly boiling." Dad had set the billy on the gas bottle stove because the campfire was in such a dire state.

David barely looked at Lisa while he sat and chatted with her parents. She was partly relieved and partly miffed. He had Mum and Dad laughing as he told them about the leaking roof in his bungalow at the back of his parent's farmhouse.

"I didn't need to fill the sink for the dishes this morning," he said. "It had filled from the drip in the ceiling. And I had to put a bucket under the one in my bedroom. Luckily it's not near the bed."

After they'd drunk their tea, Mum stood up. "We need to head to the laundromat to deal with all the muddy laundry from yesterday. Come on Lisa."

"Oh Mum, do I have to come? Can't I stay here?"

"You know I don't like you out here on your own."

"I'm fine Mum, I'm not a child!"

"I could keep Lisa company for a while if you like?" said David. He turned to Lisa, "Have you got a pack of cards? I can show you a cool trick if you like?"

"Can he, Dad?"

"Well only if you're sure, Dave, don't let us hold you up from anything."

David shook his head and grinned. "Nah, it's fine."

That morning in the train carriage David and Lisa chatted and laughed and he taught her to shuffle the deck of cards like they do in the movies. Even a couple of simple card tricks.

When Mum and Dad returned David said goodbye to them and Lisa walked with him down the long winding drive to the road.

"That's my bungalow," he pointed to the little fibro outbuilding just visible at the back of the farmhouse. "Come and visit anytime. Oh, and that's my mum." He waved to a woman peering through the farmhouse window.

"See you around, I hope," he said as he closed the gate behind him.

"See ya," said Lisa. She hoped that the rising heat in her face hadn't been as noticeable as it felt.

She strolled back towards where her parents were hanging up washing on the makeshift line strung between a couple of gums. Not far from the carriage, somewhat submerged in a massive puddle, was what had once been Lisa's boat. She fished it out with a long stick. It was now just a soggy clump of paper with inky smudges.

Over the next weeks, David started turning up at the train carriage soon after her parents had driven off somewhere. He and Lisa played cards and talked about books and as time went on Lisa opened up about feeling alone and friendless in this new place. David lent her his copy of *The Little Prince* and they watched sunsets together and quoted the Little Prince's wisdom. And at night, as she sat at the campfire with her parents, she looked to the stars and imagined him looking at them too.

As that long hot summer wore on, Lisa became more comfortable with David. He wasn't like any of the boys at her old school, or her fumbling first boyfriends with their groping hands and teeth-clacking, breath-devouring kisses.

One morning in January, when the day threatened to be sweltering by noon, she ventured across the road carrying a gift she'd been working on in the evenings. David's fibro bungalow wasn't much more than a box with cracked louvre windows and an ill-fitting door. It sat crookedly behind the farmhouse next to his old green Range Rover and a yellow gum the bark of which was stripped and scattered in a clump at its base like discarded clothes.

Lisa knocked on the door.

"Come in," David called.

Lisa pushed the door open and stepped into the tiny kitchen with its table and solitary chair.

"I'm in here."

She walked through to a curtained-off room. "I won't bite," he said as she pushed open the curtain.

He sat up in bed, smiling, his chest bare. And those bluest of blue eyes. Lisa's stomach lurched and she felt the heat rise in her cheeks.

"What would your folks say if they knew you were here and I was naked?"

"I..."

"Don't worry," he laughed, "I'm getting up."

Lisa darted back through the curtain into the kitchen. She could hear him put on his jeans. He was pulling up the zip as he stepped through the curtain.

"Tea?" He filled the kettle from the tap.

She nodded.

"What have you got there?"

Her cheeks felt hotter still. She was sure he'd think it was stupid.

"I...I made it," She shoved the box forward with her eyes focussed on some crumbs under the table. "It's for you."

She stole a glance at his face. He was smiling.

He dried his hands on his jeans and reached for the box. "Ha! It's the Little Prince's sheep in its box."

The box had three holes cut out on the side – just like in the illustration in the book. Inside was a hand-knitted sheep - made by candlelight in the train carriage from hand-spun wool.

Her heart was thumping so loud she was sure he could hear it.

He lifted her chin with his finger and looked directly into her eyes, "Thank you Lisa, it's wonderful. I love it."

She couldn't help grinning.

He put the box on the table and busied himself making tea.

"Do you want to go to a picnic this weekend? I'm meeting up with a group of kids. Some of them are from the high school."

"Yeah, ok," Lisa was leaping inside but tried to maintain a bit of cool. "I'll have to ask my folks, though."

"I can come back with you after our cup of tea to do that if you like?"

"No, I better go alone – I didn't tell them I was coming over here. Just said I was going for a walk in the bush."

David raised his eyebrows and smiled, "Right then."

It wasn't until the day before the picnic that Lisa found the courage to ask her parents if she could go. If she asked her mum, she'd no doubt say, 'ask your father', so she waited until they were together. After dinner that night she cleared and washed the dishes without being asked and made a pot of tea, ignoring the sideways glances Mum and Dad were giving to each other.

"OK love," Dad said eventually. "What is it? What do you want?"

"Well," she said. "There's a picnic tomorrow night. David

asked if I'd like to go. A bunch of kids from the high school are going to be there. He thought I might like to meet some of them before term starts."

"And where is this picnic?" Dad had his stern face on.

"Shadbolts – you know – that picnic ground up the road."

"I don't know." Dad rubbed his chin. "We don't know anything about them."

"You know David, Dad."

"Will there be drinking?"

"Dad! No...of course not."

"How do you know?'

"Well... even if there is I wouldn't have any. When have I ever..."

"We do trust you, love – that's not the point. You don't know what the other kids might get up to when they're drunk."

Mum put her hand on Dad's knee. "It might be good for her, Brian. She needs to get out and meet some of the local kids. I'm sure David will keep an eye on her. He seems like a decent fellow."

"Please Dad!"

"If your mum thinks it's OK, I guess it's OK with me – what time?"

"David said they'd pick me up at the gate at seven o'clock."

Dad looked at Mum with his eyebrows raised. She nodded.

"OK, but you make sure you're home by eleven."

Lisa hugged her dad. "Thanks – you're the best."

"What about me?" said Mum, laughing.

If they were living in a proper house, Lisa might have taken an age to get ready for the picnic, trying to do something with her unruly hair. But train carriage life meant no bathroom. They had to go to a caravan park for showers every few days and in between times washed in a bowl on a stump of wood with water that Dad carted in from Eaglehawk. There was a portable toilet in a makeshift shelter of star pickets with a corrugated iron roof and hessian walls.

Lisa took a quick glance in the small cracked square of mirror on the side of the communal wardrobe. She tied her hair back with a rubber band and, giving her parents a quick hug each, traipsed off down the drive.

David came out of his driveway as Lisa was closing the gate behind her. He pulled up in the middle of the road, leant across and pushed open the passenger door for her. "Hi there neighbour!"

She climbed in. "Where are the others?"

"They're meeting us there."

Lisa was thrilled that she had him to herself for a while. She was also anxious about meeting the local kids.

The dirt road was badly corrugated since the big rain. It had dried out quickly in the hot weather but David's car was much more comfortable than Dad's old Land Rover and they sailed over the bumps without too much discomfort.

A Kombi van was leaving as they pulled into Shadbolts. There was no-one else there.

"Looks like it's just us for now," David grinned at Lisa as they got out of the car.

He opened the back and they sat on a blanket spread on the tailgate. He opened a picnic basket and took out a bag of potato chips. They'd eaten their way through the chips and half the sandwiches and it was still just the two of them.

"Actually, I never got around to asking the others," David said. "I hope you don't mind. I can take you home if you want."

"No, it's fine." Her insides were doing backflips. She was both excited and nervous about what an evening alone with David might involve.

"Walk?" he said.

They followed the path for a while. The heat was falling

away from the day and the sky was showing the pinks and oranges of a summer sunset. The leaf litter under the old gums was crackling dry – it would burn to a crisp and devour the forest if it had a chance.

"'One loves a sunset when one is so sad'," David quoted *The Little Prince*.

"Are you sad?" she asked.

"Sometimes," he stopped and grabbed her hand, "but not right now."

They held hands walking back to the picnic ground where they sat in the back of the car with their legs stretched out on the tailgate. David pulled a bottle of wine out of the basket and two tin mugs. He poured a little into each and passed one to Lisa.

"Here's to us." David clinked his cup against hers. "I hope you like it."

She didn't like it at all. It was sweet and odd tasting and she had to force herself to swallow. But she did and took another sip. She didn't want to appear as innocent as she was. They chatted and laughed and David sat closer until they were sitting side by side as the sunset died and the moonlight took over.

David put his arm around her shoulder and she felt light

and heady and her heart was beating too fast. They sat like that and he told her about the star constellations and they laughed as they looked for asteroid B612 – the Little Prince's planet – and imagined him tending his rose there.

The moon was high in the sky when Lisa woke. "What's the time?"

David unwrapped his arm from her shoulder and checked his watch. "Shit – it's 12.30. I better get you home or your dad will kill me."

The moon gave the picnic ground an eerie patina. Silent roos grazed, looking up long enough to see they were no threat before returning to their midnight feast.

Lisa jumped down from the tailgate and stretched her legs. David reached for her and pulled her to him. He leant down and pressed his lips to hers. His stubbly chin took her by surprise and she pulled away from its scratchiness.

"Lisa?" David gripped her upper arm firmly and drew her to him again.

Her heart pounded and her stomach churned. When he kissed her again, she tried to pull away but he held the back of her head.

David only loosened his grip at the sound of a car

changing gears on the road. Headlights soon lit up the picnic ground. The kangaroos bounded away, and Lisa froze.

"Oh shit!" she said.

Her dad's Land Rover pulled up and he flung open the door. He leapt out of his seat. "I said home by eleven. Your mother's worried sick."

"I…"

David stepped forward, "Sorry Brian, we–"

Dad stabbed his finger at David's chest. "And you – what the hell is your game? Where are the others? The school kids?"

"Dad!"

"Lisa, get in the Land Rover!"

"They…they just left," David said. "We were about to head back."

Lisa did as she was told, embarrassed and confused.

"I didn't pass any other cars."

David held his hands in front of him like in a movie hold-up. "Brian–"

"What do you think you're doing out here at this time of night with a fourteen-year-old girl? Why don't you hang out with people your own age?"

Lisa felt the heat explode in her cheeks and was glad she couldn't be seen.

"Age doesn't mean a thing when you're in love." David dropped his hands.

"In love?" Dad shook his head. "Are you a sicko? She's a child and you're what? Twenty-four? Twenty-five? You should be locked up. Get the hell out of here and keep away from my daughter."

Dad had forbidden her to see David again so she waited for her parents to be out collecting wood the next day. She had his copy of *The Little Prince* with her to give back to him.

Lisa pushed open the door of his bungalow – she'd called out and knocked but there had been no answer. The kitchen table was bare, with the solitary chair tucked underneath. A motley collection of dishes were draining on the sink.

"David?" she said as she pulled aside the curtain to the bedroom. The mattress lay bare on the bedframe. The door to the tiny wardrobe lay open with a handful of metal coat hangers hanging forlornly inside. She held her breath and opened the door into the bathroom. It was empty except for a discarded towel on the floor and a smear of toothpaste in the basin.

Lisa stepped outside and closed the bungalow door.

"He's gone, love."

Lisa jumped.

David's elderly mother stood outside the door.

"Sorry, didn't mean to startle you. Oh love, did he give that book to you too?" She reached towards *The Little Prince.*

Lisa pulled the book closer to her chest.

"I thought he'd stopped all that after the last trouble. He's gone up North – never stays long here. Few months then he's up and gone. We don't see him again for ages."

Lisa couldn't speak. She turned and ran home.

2016

Lisa traced David's name, scrawled on the inside cover of the book, with her finger.

"Creepy bastard," she said. Not all predators had been as easily recognisable to her young self as a carload of drunk hoons. She wished she'd thanked her dad for turning up at Shadbolts that night, instead of paying out on him for so long afterwards. She closed the book and put it back on the shelf, scattering a multitude of memories.

Outside, the trees were whispering in the breeze and there was a slither in the leaf litter that she hoped was a lizard. A pair of magpies were squawking in a tone that bore no resemblance to their earlier tuneful warbling.

She slipped back through the fence and onto the road, pausing briefly to look across at the tiny box-like bungalow still crookedly standing behind the farmhouse, sagging with its peeling paint and rusted roof.

Lisa got into her car and headed back out of the Whipstick, the dust obscuring the vision in her rear-view mirror.

Next to her in the passenger seat was the backpack containing the ashes of her parents. They would be perfectly fine on the mantelpiece for now.

•

Turning Stones
Éireann Nankivell

THE scent of ironbark overwhelmed her other senses as slivers dislodged under her blade. All that existed was the movement of the axe in its downward trajectory and the wood sap as it was released into the air. It was the smell of eucalypt trapped in resin, the smell of bushfire, red clay, and something undefined, something sweet. Decay.

She paused, pulled at her woollen jumper, feeling sweat on her spine in the cold air. Without the sound of her axe, the bush clearing was silent. Helena wiped at a droplet on her cheek – and it was cold, close to the temperature of ice. If it rained, she would need to abandon cutting the fallen trees in the clearing into manageable chunks of firewood. Two trees had already been dismembered and this third could wait until next year.

She shifted her stance and brought the axe overhead, preparing another strike. The strike was useless, a glancing cut which nicked the wood but did not split it. A sudden needle of pain in her foot, low down in her boot, had disrupted her flow. A splinter probably, working its way into her sock. She sat on the edge of the trailer bed behind her, jiggling her left boot loose.

And stopped.

Across the clearing was a strange hash of twigs and branches, piled against the bole of a lone ironbark.

Helena got up slowly. She'd been in this clearing every day that week for a couple of hours each morning but had not seen this odd pile of branches, a huge nest built by an otherworldly bird.

Her approach was circuitous, cautious. She shuffled over the leaf litter, afraid her movements would cause the mirage to melt back into the trees. Closer, the twigs became a skeletal figure. A femur, a yellowed rib, leached with red clay, the dark eye sockets containing nothing. A few remnants of cloth hung in strips from the skeletal remains. It was difficult to determine how long the remains had been there. The clothing was deteriorated beyond recognition - had it been a plaid shirt, a trimmed bodice, an oilskin coat, a yellow windbreaker? Not even the shoes remained – the feet were bare, as though the owner had removed his slippers before turning in for the night.

The world felt strange, like the first few moments of watching a televised disaster unfolding in a familiar place. As though the event had always happened, biding its time to resolve in memory.

Helena did not want to touch this relic. She was an intruder, bringing noise and destruction in her wake. She studied the bones, committing them to memory, then pulled a map from her pocket and marked the place with her thumb nail, the impression on the paper just deep enough to see when she bent the paper in the light.

It was ANZAC day. In the morning, Helena disciplined herself to plough through her Form 6 homework at the kitchen table, alongside her dad who diligently examined his students' half-hearted science reports, his red pen moving over the papers with a tick or a cross, or to add a little note of encouragement. After lunch, he suggested, they should go bush.

She changed out of her pyjamas into her bush gear; an old pair of army surplus khakis and a scratchy jumper filled with darned-up holes in different shades. If her mother had seen her, she'd have told her to burn the outfit. Lately she'd had a penchant for telling Helena she'd never find a husband, dressed as she was. No outfit seemed to be the husband-attracting kind, but Helena was unconcerned. Her mother spent the afternoons in the darkened living room, having a lie-down, so Helena was safe from remonstrance.

They took her father's Datsun and headed out along the Eaglehawk-Neilborough Road.

"Let's go out to Old Tom," she said.

Gavin gave his daughter a sideward glance. "You promise you won't go into the mine, if I take us there?"

"Dad, it's fine, I know to be careful."

He sighed. "Last time we went, that shaft looked to be deteriorating. Don't go in, Helena. Okay?"

She nodded and he turned the car off the sealed road, nosing over a ditch and onto the dirt road.

Gavin had brought his field equipment—notebooks, soil temperature gauge, a bundle of thermometers labelled 'Eaglehawk High School', her mother's coiled sewing tape.

"The mullock heap is a good place to start anyway," he said. She looked toward the greying pile of stone that stood beside the rusted poppet head. The poppet had begun to look like a crouched old woman of late; bent by the weight of her years she was ready to collapse back to the earth.

They walked with care between the ironbarks, heads bent to survey the ground for newly-revealed ventilation shafts or old diggings that had been improperly back-filled. Below their feet was a Swiss cheese of mine works and tunnels, reaching into the earth.

Helena was fascinated by the mines. Not the prospect of gold, like the old shades she often saw meandering between the gums, grasping metal detectors and listening for the eerie whistles relayed from their instruments to their headphones. She was interested in what the mines laid bare; stratum of rock, the surface chiseled back to show the folded feldspar and quartz, the quartz pushing through the feldspar parent rock like a river, as it had once been, molten silica forced from deeper underground.

Her dad was interested in what lay under some specific rocks – the pink-tailed worm lizard. These thin-bodied legless lizards looked like huge earthworms to the untrained eye, or tiny snakes. He came regularly to the Whipstick to track the species and document population and habitat, in the hopes of writing a report which would garner government interest in protecting the species.

At the mullock heap they began to methodically search. The lizard preferred dinner-plate-sized rocks an inch or so thick. They lived in ant burrows, eating ants. Turning stones was slow work because if either uncovered signs of an ant hill beneath, they would measure the soil and air temperature where the stone was, Gavin making notations.

"I'm going to go check under the rocks up the hill," Gavin said, once much of the mullock heap had been turned with no sign of their quarry. Sometimes on their Whipstick expeditions they saw no worm-lizards, coming home covered in red dust without a triumph to shield them from her mother's scolding over their state of dirtiness.

"Ok, I'm going to keep looking here," she said.

She watched his retreat along a roo track, his plaid shirt mingling with the colours of the bush as he was gradually lost to sight. She turned rocks for a few more minutes just to be on the safe side, in case he could still hear the thud of stone as she pried it loose and it skidded down the heap.

The entrance to Old Tom was called an 'adit', extending horizontally about fifty feet into the earth before the decline began in earnest. She'd explored the tunnel before on several occasions with her father, but he cautioned against exploring the decline beyond. If she was only gone ten minutes, her father need never know she'd been further in. She didn't want to worry him.

From her back pocket, she pulled a torch with a weak

yellow beam. The adit was smooth underfoot, but from the mouth of the decline became uneven. She braced herself, leaning back as she descended, her feet angled to maintain balance and give her shoes more to grip. She traced her hands over the walls, abrading her skin on the blasted rock. She could distinguish the feldspar, and how it differed from quartz, even without directing her torch to the wall. The feldspar was grainier, dry to touch due to the multitude of fine pores in the stone. The quartz was rough with a silky texture, because of the high silica content. She was pleased with her knowledge, her connection to the rock.

The decline flattened into another horizontal section, extending ten feet before another tunnel led to further darkness. Her torch struggled to cast its beam into the whole of the dark space ahead. Behind her, she heard gravel slither underfoot, her father's voice calling to her.

She turned towards the entrance, aiming the torch up into the tunnel. As she turned, a stone the size of her fist crashed into her shin, set loose as her dad slid along the decline, puffing and cursing in low tones which echoed in the space. She yelped and stepped backward. Her left foot was now resting on a surface that was not rock. It was a wooden beam, desiccated in the dry air of the mine.

What an idiot she'd been, to think her dad wouldn't notice she'd left the mullock heap. He was too wary of the pull the mines had on her to leave her alone long.

She took another step back, her whole weight on the beam, just as Gavin appeared. His head lamp projected a powerful light across her face, momentarily dazzling her.

The beam creaked again, a lengthy groan.

"Helena!"

The beam was flexing under her weight, strained after years of lying untouched underground. She was paralysed in her dad's headlamp.

Gavin must have heard the creaking too. His hand darted to her upper arm and took a firm grip, and he dragged her toward him. Even as she was pulled away, she felt the collapse of the beam, the sudden nothingness under the soles of her shoes, a weightless scrabbling as her father embraced her.

"Jesus," said Gavin. He directed his head lamp to the floor, revealing the remaining wooden beams covering a shaft, and a black rectilinear hole.

Helena sat down. She felt sick. Her temples throbbed

with blood and panic, her veins thrummed with anxious energy. How easily she could have disappeared into that hole, if her father had not come at the exact moment he did?

Gavin got onto his stomach, inching out near the hole. He dropped a rock into the gap, but they heard no sound.

"Old Tom's eleven hundred feet deep," he said. He did not sound angry, only sad. He was looking at her, but she couldn't see his expression, because the head lamp was blinding, and her eyes were stinging with quartz dust.

It wasn't unusual for Gavin to be late back when he went hunting for the worm-lizard, because he liked to track their activities at dusk. If it was late or he wanted to be in the forest before dawn, he'd kip in his sleeping bag at the cabin. So at first there was no alarm. She'd gone to bed expecting to see her father at breakfast, eating toast. And her mother was too wrapped in her own concerns.

It was the next afternoon when they called the police to report him missing. Groups of men combed the Whipstick in the areas Helena said he frequented, carrying sticks in front of their bodies to test the stability of the earth as they advanced.

Within days the consensus was her father was at the bottom

of a shaft. For the first two days there was hope he might be calling for help, and the searchers could be rescuers. That final afternoon in the Whipstick became like a diorama enclosed in glass, trapped in stillness for all eternity.

Helena sat at the formica table, looking out on to the forest before dawn. Soon there would be birdsong, and the trees would change their clothes from ink to thickened bark.

The cabin was nothing special, the cheap fibro her dad had assembled more than forty years ago. It sat on property her family had owned for decades off Skylark Road in the Whipstick State Forest, one of only a few freehold properties left in the reserve. The road to the cabin was a roo track, widened under the wheels of her Pajero. Before her dad disappeared, the cabin had been a base of operations. Somewhere for Gavin to assemble his notes, pin his detailed botanical drawings to the walls. Helena had relished the few times when she and her father had stayed overnight here to get an early start in the forest. Now she looked at the grubby wood stove, the rust spots on the legs of the fold-out chairs that served double lives as dining chairs and lounge suite. She noticed the paint peeling on the walls where sunlight shone through the windows. Gavin's drawings had long been taken down and stored away.

Her adult children had begged her to come back in to Bendigo. She had begun living here when she separated from her husband, after she won a contract with a mining company for a geological survey to determine the viability of taking gold from the old mines.

It was a bet against herself. The money was necessary, and despite her reservations about taking a contract that may do the Whipstick harm, it seemed unlikely there would be gold left to warrant the expense of petitioning to mine in a state reserve. Her own nature would not allow her to falsify her findings. If the sites had shown themselves valuable, she would be morally bound to include it in her report.

She found the crate of her dad's old notebooks. There was still a thermometer in the crate, the faded label declaiming itself as property of Eaglehawk High. She didn't know what she was looking for in the notes. Just some sign to tell her what to do. The notebooks weren't a diary; occasionally Gavin had scribbled lines for the report he was working on at the bottom of a page of recordings. No recording of his personal life, no hint about his strong affiliation with the

Whipstick and his desire for its preservation. Just scientific data, obtuse and now roughly meaningless.

She had perused the same notes years ago. In the early days after Gavin disappeared, she wondered if he really was swallowed by a mine shaft. Her dad was knowledgeable about the area. Maybe he'd left them, left the bickering between himself and her mother behind, in search of solitude to complete his works. The notebooks were impassive then, as they were now.

The morning passed in silent reflection. She took slow walks around the block, kicking the rocks that constituted her livelihood. On the bush block, her solitary lifestyle seemed natural. The thought of returning to her Edwardian house in town, silent but for the traffic outside, seemed much lonelier.

Now it was time.

The indent she'd made with her thumbnail was still visible on the map. She traced the mark with a pen, just to be sure. She'd avoided that particular location. She'd found another spot to cut wood for the encroaching winter.

Was it a police matter? She wasn't sure. A skeleton was a dead person. Finding the dead usually involved the police in the first instance.

The cop at the desk was tapping on a keyboard when she entered. She cleared her throat.

"Excuse me, I don't know if this is something you deal with, but I've found something in the Whipstick." Her voice sounded overly-refined to her own ears, like a disgusted school marm who'd stepped in dog poop. She coughed.

"What type of something?"

"Some bones, I think they might be human. I am happy to show them to you." She held out the map.

"Well, not to me personally, I'll get one of our detectives in from the Bendigo station to go with you." As he made a phone call, Helena did a tour of the tiny station, studying the photographs of former captains, police sports teams, framed medals for service.

"If you want to wait here, a detective will be along in about half an hour or so."

When the detective arrived, they shook hands.

"We'll take my car and you can direct me to this find," the woman said.

"We could take my Pajero, it's a little off-road."

"I prefer to take the police vehicle. I'll follow you."

Helena watched in the rearview mirror as the detective's car peeled out from the curb, following the Pajero. The Pajero was accustomed to the dirt roads in the Whipstick, but the detective's Toyota hybrid was out of place. Red dust was accumulating on the lower exterior as the cars bounced along the track.

She stopped twenty metres from the clearing and waited as the detective gathered her phone and notebook from the console.

The two women strode in silence, lifting their feet in unison to pass a fallen branch, picking their way between the understory of coffee bush.

Helena paused, unsure. The clearing was the same as she'd seen it last, when she was axing the fallen trees three weeks ago. The same massive ironbark lay in the middle of the clearing, her axe marks criss-crossing its marrow. The imprints from her trailer tyres in the mud were undisturbed. The air had body to it, viscous like imminent tears. She turned toward the bole of the ironbark, looking for the tangle of bones she had thought a strange offering to the trees, and was greeted with emptiness. No skull peered back.

"Can you point out the remains, Helena?" The detective seemed to sense her shock. The' young woman was scanning the clearing with her head tilted, like a bird.

"I... no, well, the bones were here." She gestured to the lone ironbark.

The detective strode towards it, still scanning, her eyes intent on recognising some sign of disturbance. She crouched beside the base of the tree, levering her pen under a sodden piece of cloth.

"How long ago did you see the remains?"

"About three weeks ago. I wasn't sure what to do."

The detective made a pensive sound in the back of her throat. "I can't see anything here that appears to be bone. Are you positive this is the location?"

Helena saw vividly her own thumbnail as it marked this spot. She nodded.

The detective shrugged. Her gaze lingered on Helena's.

"I'm sorry, this seems to have wasted your time," Helena said. Her eyes were hot beneath the lids, her cheeks flushed. If she wiped her tears, the whole of the Whipstick might be wiped away with them.

"No harm done. Perhaps if you come across remains again you'd best call it in immediately. I'll leave you now."

The clearing felt like absence after the detective's departure. Beyond the clearing, the voids between the trees seemed to grow and contract as she watched, the trees breathing as one in slow rhythm. Helena thought of the times she had come here with her father, as a child and then a teenager. The forest was always a harsh landscape, hostile to wary visitors who did not take care of the mine shafts. Her father's fibro shack had been their refuge, always threatened by the hungry forest.

Somewhere between the trees the wind whipped up, scattering plumes of fine-grained red dust through the Whipstick, scattering the faith she had that her father was out here, stalking between the yellow gums and mullock heaps, hunting worm-lizards, waiting for her to bring him home.

•

Lizard Land
Mary Pomfret

HIS tooth had been bothering him all day but Lizard hadn't let on. He slung his backpack over his shoulder, cupped his hand around his jaw and walked into the quiet shadowy depths of the Whipstick forest. The battered old bag held most of what any man could ever need. Matches — never got too far without matches. Good length of rope. Never know when you might need rope. Can opener. Bottle opener. A half roll of toilet paper. Tobacco. Cigarette papers. And a magazine cutting of a blonde woman with red lips and a dazzling smile, like she had diamonds in her teeth. He'd have to get a frame for it one day. It mightn't have actually been his mother, but he reckoned she might look something like her. Who knows, it *might* even have been his mum. His tooth sure was throbbing. Tomorrow, he'd ask the boss where he kept the pliers

He walked on down the dirt track. He knew if he looked back his long shadow would be behind him. Made him feel less lonely, somehow. One thing he liked about the Whipstick was that he was always finding stuff. Only yesterday, he'd picked up a pair of Ray-Bans. Some poor bugger must have dropped them. Too bad. His now. He pushed them up his nose. Wasn't that he wanted to take other people's things. Just that he reckoned his need might have been greater. He'd spotted a good mattress down the track. Been there a while. Cops had put crime tape around it. Crime tape. What a joke. Cops hated people dumping their rubbish in the bush. Could be a bit risky though, so he probably wouldn't try and take it yet. But he was happy with the Nike joggers he'd picked up a while back. Couple of sizes too small, but he was stretching them. Each night he put them on and he'd wear them a little bit longer each time. He'd get there. Make them fit. Brand new shoes—too good to waste. He'd put them on again tonight. Once the fire was going and the baked beans were in the pot, he'd put on some other bloke's shoes. Could have belonged to the same bloke who dropped the Ray-Bans.

Not far to go now, to the hut. Must have been a miners' hut or something, once. His home now, or at least, for the time being anyway. Shelter was shelter. He trudged along the path. Always good to keep your eyes down. Never know what else you might find. He liked the ochre-coloured dust. Made him feel at home, like he blended in with the landscape somehow, with his red hair, freckles and scaly skin. The boss told him he should go to the doctor's and get checked out for skin cancer. But you had to have one of them Medicare cards to go to the doctors. He didn't have one of those. You needed a birth certificate for that. And he didn't have one of those either. The Department said they would give him one as soon as he left the foster home, but he never got around to collecting it. They weren't too bad, Mr and Mrs Blewitt; but they weren't too good either. They'd fed him at least. Well, most of the time. He tried not to think of them ever, if he could help it. He knew his real name. James. James Border. Mrs Blewitt had told him that. But whenever anyone asked him his name he said, "I'm Lizard, to my mates."

Two months it'd been now, working for the boss on the block out of town, humping bricks and digging dirt and living at the hut. But he had his own swag, his iron pot, tin billy-can and his enamel mug. Each morning, before he left for the block, he made sure all his things were neatly stacked. He liked things to be tidy.

The tooth was really starting to give him curry. But he still had a good half a flask of Bundy hidden behind the hut. A few good swigs would dull the pain. He felt inside his pocket. Still three Panadol left—he'd nicked them from the medicine chest at work. He walked on. Misshapen ironbarks cast dark silhouettes and spindly branches criss-crossed in front of him on the narrowing path leading to the hut. His own long shadow followed him. Nearly there. Just around the bend.

He stopped. Dead still. The door was open. Wide open.

Bending low on his haunches, leaning forward, eyes focussed on the open door, he crept down the path. He didn't see the empty coke can in front of him. The crunch made his stomach lurch. "Shush," he whispered to no one. He stepped slowly through the doorway.

"The stinking bastards,' he yelled. 'The stinking rotten bastards."

Loser Cunt Dog. Red paint. The words hung on the corrugated iron like open wounds. The paint smell permeated the hut. His cast iron pot, billy can and his enamel mug weren't neatly stacked in the corner with the jar of coffee where he had left them. The vandals had emptied out a near-full jar of coffee. Fuckers. He'd only bought it yesterday and he was going to make it last a good month. And his pot, his billycan and his enamel cup were sitting in the middle of the dirt floor. He smelt the strong odour of urine. He bent down and, one by one, hurled his cookware out the door, the yellow piss splashing back at him in the wind. "If you come back here again, I'll fucken kill you," he yelled. He had that choking feeling in his throat like he was going to cry. But he wouldn't cry. "Mongrels. Mongrel dogs."

He'd have to move. He couldn't stay here now. They'd be back. He looked around the hut. It could have been worse. At least they hadn't touched his swag. Morons probably didn't even know what it was. And they hadn't found the Bundy. Well, he'd spend one more night here and head off at first light. He'd have to find somewhere else. The smell of the paint was so strong, he'd have to leave the door open all night. Either that or choke on the fumes

Outside the hut, he paced up and down, shouting profanities, kicking his boot against the dirt and hurling rocks at the tree trunks as hard as he could, shattering the silence of the darkening timberland. A savage rage took him over sometimes, hard and wild, and turned him into someone else. All the while he was yelling and cursing, he hadn't realised that the sun had already set and night had fallen silently in the forest.

Exhausted, he gathered a few sticks and branches and made a small fire in the ashes from the night before. Wouldn't worry about heating up the baked beans. Those mongrel kids had pissed in his cooking pot and he didn't want to waste his water washing it. He'd just drink the Bundy from the flask and take the three Panadol. He'd forgotten about his toothache until he sat down next to the struggling flames. A cold wind blew through the forest and he couldn't even be bothered looking for more leaves to stoke the fire. He sculled the rum. The sweet syrupy liquid burnt the back of his throat and the warmth radiated through his body, down his arms and to his fingertips. When he'd drained the last drop of Bundy, he shovelled dirt on to the fire and crawled into the hut, rolled out his swag and fell into a thick drunken sleep.

Somewhere between midnight and dawn, rain began to pelt down on the roof of the hut. He raised his head and cupped his jaw with his hand. Water was leaking in on him through the cracks. He'd been meaning to do something about the holes, but he just hadn't gotten around to it. It must have been raining for a while, because he could see a small puddle on the dirt floor. The moonlight shone in though the open door and the wind howled. But he was too done in to get up and move his swag to the dry corner. He fell back into a deep stupor. About an hour later he woke again. His tooth was aching so much it took him a moment or two to register the depth of the pain. The rain had stopped but his swag was sodden and his coat was wet through. Belly retching from hunger and rum. Whole body shivering.

There'd been times before when he'd thought of giving up. Packing it all in. Thinking he was done. Usually in the middle of the night when the loneliness of it all closed in on him, but he always managed to beat it somehow. And he never cried. Not once. Times before he'd always been able to hang on till he heard the first morning magpie, but tonight he wondered if this was going to be it. Finally.

The wet coat was heavy on his chest. Made him think of the time a kid had punched him in the face, knocked him down in the school yard, and sat on him. He remembered, too, that old Mrs Blewitt had yelled at him when he got home for ripping his shirt and fighting and carrying on like a heathen. 'There'll be no tea for you tonight, my lad.' He remembered lying in his cold bed hungry with his jaw aching just like it was tonight. Must have been that stupid old bugger Mr Blewitt who had christened him *Lizard*. Drunken old bastard. Couldn't remember anyone ever calling him James. As soon as he turned sixteen the Blewitts had turfed him out and he'd caught a bus up to Alice Springs. The station-hand job wasn't too bad. Three meals a day and a bed. And he stayed on. Sometimes he would go into Alice for a bender. Usually he got beat up or arrested but eventually he would make his way back to the cattle station. He remembered one day the station cook asked him when his birthday was. Well, she'd said, if you could find out I will make you a birthday cake for your next one. He never could remember having a birthday cake or even a birthday. Cooks came and went and the hot dusty years floated by. One day, not long after the old man died, the missus called all the staff into the kitchen.

She'd sold the station to some bloke from Shanghai. She was sorry but they all had to be off the place by the end of the month. He'd guessed the five hundred dollars extra in his pay packet was for long service leave or something. The closest thing to a thankyou he'd ever had. And after that he'd just drifted. Taken whatever he could find, wherever he could find it.

It'd be easier to go now, in so many ways. He'd hung on for so long. Forty years he'd managed to stay alive, or at least he supposed it was something like forty years. He'd lost count. If he let go now, he wouldn't have to go and wait on the side of the road for the boss in the freezing cold anymore. No more working all day on an empty stomach if the boss didn't bring sandwiches. He wouldn't have to think about when he could afford to pay for a woman again. That's the only kind of woman he'd ever had. Once, he even paid extra for kissing. He was sick of it. Sick of the uselessness of it all. He leaned over and reached inside his backpack. He pulled out the rope and ran it through the crease of his palm. Smooth. A bloke he'd known who'd been inside showed him how to tie a noose. The wind whistled in the open door. He'd had enough. Anyhow who'd miss him?

He sat up and leaned his back against the rusty iron wall.

Nothing colder in the middle of the night than corrugated iron. Well, he always knew that he was going to do it one day. He'd reached the fucken end of the line. And he never cried. Mrs Blewitt saw to that. "Big boys don't cry. Don't come whinging around me you snivelling little brat." If he even looked like he was going to cry, Mrs Blewitt would give him a backhander right across the face. "Stuff you, you miserable old crow," he screeched into the black night. He stood up with the rope in his hand and began to stagger towards the doorway.

Then, something small and quick scampered in front of him to the far corner of the hut. Green eyes glistened in the moonlight, staring. A fox? A little closer. A dark thing. The dark thing began to wail. A sorrowful high-pitched wail. "What the?" The matted furry thing cowered in the corner and hissed, back arched.

He dropped his rope at his side and picked up the wet ball of fur. He held it in the palm of his hand. Kitten. Wet through. Trembling . Tiny. He reached and pulled an old T-shirt from his backpack and began to pat the kitten dry: ever so gently. He didn't want to frighten it more than it already was. But the more he dried its muddy knotted coat, the more the little thing howled. He stepped out of the hut leaving the length of rope coiled on the floor behind him. He stuffed the kitten inside his jumper and it stopped wailing. The kitten purred and purred. He stood in front of the hut and watched the sun begin to rise on the dark horizon.

The rain had stopped and the air was sweet and fresh. The kitten crawled up his chest and nestled around his neck and rubbed its wet nose against his skin. The kitten's purring vibrated in his ear and something within him shifted, opened up, like a seed bursting its shell. The tightness in his throat loosened. Tears began to flow. He squeezed his eyes shut, but he couldn't stop the tears flooding and flowing freely down his cheeks. With one hand holding the kitten to him, he sank to his knees on the forest floor. His shoulders began to shake. In the bright morning sunlight, he began crying all he had held inside for so long, as if he would never stop.

A magpie warbled its first morning song. And a new day broke over the Whipstick.

•

The Claim
Bridget Robertson

HAMISH O' Dowd pushed through the canvas opening of his tent and stepped into the darkness of early morning. Smoke from last night's campfires drifted through the scrub, giving the bony eucalypts a chalky, ghost-like appearance. He collected a handful of kindling and poked at the ash pit in front of the tent. When a small flame caught alight he picked up two large branches and crisscrossed them over the fire, before pouring the last of his water into a blackened billycan. His foot accidentally kicked something on the ground and it went clattering against the rocks – Angus's drinking cup. Hamish picked it up and held it under his nose. It smelled of something sweet. Rum.

"Goddammit." He threw it back on the ground and charged down the hill in search of his brother.

It was a short distance from the campsite to the mining claims at the bottom of Beelzebub gully. As he stepped down into the pit he felt something move under his feet. He stumbled sideways and saw it was just a long stick lying across the path. He kicked it out of the way and jumped into the shallow mine. His brother's grey blanket was on the ground, but there was no sign of him. He looked through the bushes next to the mine shaft and hissed, "Angus!"

A flock of cockatoos scattered through the trees,

answering his call with their own raucous squawking. Their wings were like tiny flags as the sky turned from a deep black to a dark indigo.

Out of the corner of his eye, he noticed movement. It was George from the neighbouring claim staggering to his feet.

"What's goin' on?"

Hamish's eyes creased as he scanned the bush. "You seen Angus?"

"He was 'ere last night for a wee while." George grinned at him. "Snuck off on ye?"

Hamish pointed at the ground. "Don't let anyone down 'ere."

"Nay I wouldn't. The night fossickers'd be long gone by now."

Hamish looked at the blanket on the ground and tilted his head towards George. "Prob'ly lucky you were 'ere last night I reckon. Can't bloody trust Angus."

Hamish glanced up the gully at his fire glowing in the distance. If he'd looked in the other direction, down the hill, he might have seen Angus's sweat rag lying on the ground between two wattle trees.

The water was almost to a boil when Hamish returned

to camp. He stepped inside the tent to find his cup next to Angus's bed, along with some dirty plates his brother had forgotten to clean up. Angus was a messer and it drove Hamish mad. He picked up the spare blanket that had fallen on the ground and something sharp stabbed his index finger – the needle and thread Angus had used the day before to darn his socks.

Hamish grimaced as he pulled it from his finger. "Angus, ya gobshite."

As the sun inched above the horizon, Hamish sat by the fire and poured hot tea into his cup. He watched Lee Sam come down the hill with two full buckets of water swinging on the ends of his shoulder pole.

"Lee!" Hamish called out.

Lee Sam gave him a quick nod, detouring off the path towards him. Hamish reached under his shirt for the leather pouch secured around his waist. His fingers brushed against a small piece of gold sewn into the waistband of his trousers. He suddenly thought about the other nuggets buried under the floor of the tent, and wondered if he should dig them up. Maybe stitch them into his trousers before he started work for the day. Just to be safe. Lee Sam unhitched the two full buckets and attached the empty ones, shaking his head at Hamish.

"Angus, him no good."

Hamish nodded. "That's about the truth of it."

Hamish pulled a shilling out of his pouch and flipped it through the air. He watched Lee's eyes widen when he threw the second one. "It's been a good week."

Lee pressed his palms together and bowed his head.

"Angus," he said again, pointing away from the camp towards the walking track. He shook his head. "No good."

Hamish lowered his eyes. "You seen him then?"

The thin ponytail hanging down Lee's back swung through the air as he turned towards the gully. He clicked his fingers for Hamish to follow.

Lee Sam led him through the claim site and past George, who narrowed his gaze at Lee. When they reached the two wattle trees Hamish saw the sweat rag lying in the dirt. Lee stopped, and spun several times looking into the forest as though he were lost.

"What is it?" Hamish asked.

Lee didn't answer. He stared blankly at Hamish before

placing his palms together.

"Sorry," he said.

"D'ye see him 'ere?" Hamish asked.

Lee Sam pointed to the ground, between the two trees.

Hamish reached down and picked up the soiled rag smudged with sweat and dirt. He scanned the bush, then shoved the rag in his pocket. "Well, he's not 'ere now."

Hamish was about to make his way up the gully when Lee called him back.

"Look."

Hamish didn't see anything at first, but heard a familiar thrum nearby. When he stepped closer to the trees he saw a swarm of flies lingering over a fold of rock, eager to get their spongy mouths on a sticky pool of blood. Then he heard footsteps behind him, and a hand slapped him on the back.

"Ye find him?" It was George.

"No." Hamish sighed. "Lee saw him 'ere." He nodded towards the trees and the blood-stained rock.

"Aye, did he now." George glared at Lee. 'Where is he then?'

Lee Sam didn't answer.

George gripped Hamish by the shoulder. "He's prob'ly drunk and passed out somewhere. I'm sure he won't be too far away."

Hamish lifted his brow. "Aye."

Angus did not appear for work all that morning. As Hamish stopped for his dinner break, he felt a rush of anger, throwing his pick down into the dirt.

When his brother did not appear between noon and one o'clock, when all miners needed to be onsite to avoid claim jumpers, dampness prickled on his skin. He looked for Angus in the camps dotted along the top of the gully. He went to Big Polly's tent, but she had not seen him since the night before.

Hamish borrowed a horse from a neighbouring campsite and galloped the six miles through mining gullies and ironbark forests to the police barracks at the top of Camp Hill to report his brother missing. Later that afternoon, a young constable and a member of the Native Police Corps dismounted their horses next to Hamish's tent.

"Constable Smyth." The taller man announced, wiping his brow with a white handkerchief. He tilted his head at the Aboriginal man next to him. "This is Freddy."

Hamish led the two men through the gully, down into the

Bushland, to the place Lee had shown him earlier that morning.

"Apparently, he was last seen 'ere."

Constable Smyth crouched to take a closer look. Freddy stood several metres away scanning the ground, carefully stepping over rocks and scattered branches. He reached down to pick something up amongst the dried leaves and bark. He held it up for the constable, who took it and turned it over in his palm several times.

Constable Smyth held his arm outstretched towards Hamish, "You recognise this?"

Dangling from his fingers was a short piece of red string with three bronze coins threaded through it.

"Looks Chinese," Hamish said.

Freddy stepped away from the two men and tipped his head towards the nearby trees. "He's been 'ere." He nodded at the wattle branches on the ground and pointed past them. "Through there."

"Can you track him?" The constable asked.

Freddy lifted his chin skyward and stepped over the blood-stained rock. They walked for almost an hour, zig-zagging between grey box trees and firethorn bushes. Mounds of loose earth were piled high where miners had been six months ago, before they had moved further up the gully.

When they reached a small clearing, Freddy stopped, and the two men paused behind him.

"You lost it?" The constable asked.

Freddy didn't answer as he walked to the top of a mullock heap. He stood for several moments, before nodding at the two men to join him.

When Hamish saw his brother's lifeless body in the bottom of the shallow mineshaft, he drew a sharp breath.

"Oh Jesus Mary," he whispered.

Angus was on his back, cobalt eyes staring blankly at the sky above them. Bloody clumps of hair stuck to his forehead and a thick film of foamy saliva had dried around his mouth. There was a bottle of rum, with less than a mouthful left in it, on the ground next to him.

"'Tis not like Angus to leave a drop." Hamish said quietly.

His throat tightened as he watched the men lift his younger brother out of the mineshaft. When they laid his body down Freddy touched his own eyelids with his fingertips, showing Hamish that he should close his brother's eyes.

In a low voice, the young constable said, "I'll go back for the horses." Beads of sweat were forming on his brow as he squinted up at the feverish sky. "We can't leave him out 'ere."

Hamish sat down heavily in the dirt, next to his brother's body, his hands shaking as he smoothed Angus's sandy hair the way his mother used to do when they were young. He had never intended that Angus should come with him to the goldfields, but his mother had begged him. She said there was no life for either of them in Ireland.

Looking at his brother's body lying in the dirt he felt a pressing weight in his chest. There was no life for them here either.

Angus O' Dowd was carried through the campsite draped over the saddle of a horse. A blanket covered his face and torso. Miners gathered to watch, holding their hats to their chests. A quiet murmuring spread through the group of men as the body passed. The horse's hooves clipped the rocky ground as Freddy held the bridle, leading the horse away from camp.

The body was taken to the Thunder Plains hotel five miles away and placed in the cool room, along with sides of beef and bottles of beer. Hamish couldn't help thinking Angus would be pleased with his surroundings. He hated the heat. He had not stopped complaining about it since they arrived three months ago. When they decided they needed to stake their own claim, their only choice was to head north of the Bendigo Creek to Elysian Flats. They soon discovered it was no Elysian landscape. When Angus heard the area was called Beelzebub Gully, he had ruefully surveyed their new surroundings.

"It's the devil's arse alright," he said.

Hamish smiled as he ran his fingers along the waistband of Angus's trousers, he couldn't feel any lumps of gold. He checked his brother's shirt, skimming his hands across the pockets and gently pressed along the material. Then he remembered the gold nuggets that were still buried beneath the canvas floor of the tent.

The priest arrived a short time later; he was a portly man whose neck bulged above the collar of his cassock. Hamish pulled a flask of rum from his coat pocket and took a long swig before handing it to the priest. The father took a small sip and coughed into the back of his hand. Hamish held the flask over his brother's head and let a small amount of rum drip onto his temple, he watched it bead down his ear and pool on the dark wooden floor. Hamish's eyes glistened as he said his last words to his brother.

"Here's to beefsteak when you're hungry,

Whisky when you're dry,

All the women you'll ever want,

And heaven when you die."

Hamish took another drink from the flask. "Go thee well brother," he whispered.

He tucked Angus's shirt into his trousers and handed the priest a waistcoat and a sprig of yellow wattle for his brother's lapel. He slipped a small gold nugget into the priest's hand. "Put him somewhere nice."

The priest furrowed his brow. "No funeral?"

"No." Hamish looked at his brother's body lying on the floor. "Nay be worth it."

As he left the hotel he glanced up at the sun's position in the sky and realised he didn't have much time.

When Hamish returned to Beelzebub Gully he could hear raised voices at the other end of the camp. As he approached he could see a group of men gathered outside his tent. Lee Sam was scurrying up the gully away from the group of miners.

George's voice pierced the air, "Get out of 'ere ye thievin' celestial."

Hamish watched Lee Sam disappear through the trees and he called out to George. "What are ye doin' man?"

"Lee was in ye tent, fishin' around." George said.

Hamish flung the flap of the tent open and pulled up the piece of canvas in the centre of the floor. He dug madly at the loose patch of dirt. His pulse quickened when he realised they weren't there. The gold nuggets were gone. "He's stolen me bloody gold!"

As Hamish flew out the door, he didn't see the pot of freshly stewed mutton and Chinese vegetables Lee had left for him.

When Hamish reached the edge of the Chinese camp, two miles west of Beelzebub Gully, he found Lee Sam working with a group of men on a mound of old mine tailings.

As Hamish approached, Lee lowered his eyes, "Sorry for Angus," he said.

Hamish didn't hear him as he rushed at the group of men. He grabbed Lee by the throat and threw him to the ground. "Where is it?" he hissed.

Lee squeezed his eyes shut several times, his pupils darting as he searched Hamish's face.

"Where's the gold?" Hamish snapped, his forearm pressing against Lee's neck. Within seconds a group of men jumped on Hamish and wrestled him to the ground. Hamish saw the glint of metal and heard the sound of a shotgun barrel snapping open.

A man with piercing dark eyes pointed a gun at his chest. "Go," he said in a flat voice.

It was difficult to sleep that night. Hamish tossed and turned as the cold ground settled in his bones. He imagined Angus buried beneath the dirt and shale wearing his good waistcoat, the wattle in his lapel and his freshly darned socks.

Hamish sat upright, rigid as a spike.

In his freshly darned socks.

After two hours of digging Hamish finally unearthed the lower half of his brother's body. Hot bile sluiced in his throat as he carefully cleaned the dirt from Angus's trousers and boots.

"Lord have mercy on me," he whispered.

He turned his head skyward as he placed his hand on his

brother's ankles and found what he was looking for. Sewn into the cuff of Angus's right sock were six pebble-sized pieces of gold. As he peeled the sock from his brother's foot, he drew a sharp breath. Angus's ankle was swollen with a blackish indigo bruise covering the lower part of his leg. When he lifted his trouser a little more he saw the two bloodied puncture marks of a snakebite.

Constable Smyth arrived in Beelzebub Gully early the next morning. He dismounted his horse in front of Hamish's tent. "The Chinese camp was attacked last night." He lifted his chin at Hamish. "Do you know anything about it?"

Hamish picked up a branch and snapped it over his knee, a wave of nausea rising and falling in his stomach.

"Did you go there last night?" The constable asked.

"No." Hamish said quietly.

"Someone set fire to one of the tents." He paused, searching Hamish's face. "Three men are dead."

Hamish stood motionless as the words sunk in. He looked over at George sitting by his own fire, blowing steam from a cup he was holding to his lips.

"It's a serious crime." The constable said. "Whoever did it, he'll hang for it."

Hamish nodded solemnly. "Aye."

The constable turned to the other miners gathered nearby. "There'll be a full investigation on what happened last night, and if there are any more problems with the Chinese, we'll shut this gully down!"

George glanced up as Hamish walked towards him, then averted his gaze back to the fire.

Hamish's breathing became shallow. "Did ye do it?"

George didn't say anything.

"Ah Jesus man!"

George's eyes glistened as he clasped his hands together. "He stole ye gold," he said.

Hamish pressed his thumb into his temple and rubbed his fingers across his forehead. "Nay he didn't," he sighed. "He didn't steal the gold."

George hung his head as Hamish explained to him what happened. When Hamish finished, George's voice cracked.

"He prob'ly would've jumped ye claim."

"Ye killed three men," Hamish hissed.

George's eyes filled with tears. "I only meant to scare em."

The following day, Hamish gathered his belongings and left his tent. He left the mineshafts, and he left the forest that claimed his brother. And he walked between the ironbark and wattle trees with six gold nuggets sewn into the cuff of his right sock.

When he arrived at the outskirts of the Chinese camp he could smell the charred remains of the burnt-out tent. Lee was sitting in a small circle with several other men when Hamish approached. Two of them stood up and Hamish held his hands out in front of him, then unhitched the pickaxe from his belongings.

"I'm sorry," Hamish held the pick towards Lee. "Take it."

Lee stood solemnly with his arms hanging by his side.

Hamish looked up at the position of the sun high above them. "Ye best be goin' if ye are to make it to the claim on time," He placed the pick in Lee's hand. "It's yours if ye want it."

•

Unfortunate Bolle's
Jennifer Walker Teh

MARNIE lay on one of the narrow beds at the back of the caravan. It was hot and perspiration made her body stick to the bed's orange vinyl cover.

In real estate terms the interior of van would be described as 'mid-century modern, in need of renovation'. In fact, it housed all its original 1970s fittings. Faded curtains, which once sported a bold geometric design of orange and brown, were now barely thick enough to cover the windows. Gold-speckled laminate on the benches had buckled where water had seeped under it. This was a far cry from Marnie's usual life.

The van began to sway then vibrate. They were on an unsealed road and she could smell the dust in the back of her nostrils. It stuck in her throat and she began to cough.

With each cough Marnie's body heaved and the ropes which tied her hands and feet cut into her skin. They were tight. It was hopeless and Marnie was petrified. There was nothing she could do now.

'Report All Suspicious Cars' read a sign at the turn towards the Whipstick. The forest closed in around the dirt road and, occasionally, decaying houses could be glimpsed between the trees. Some had outbuildings of mismatched corrugated iron and old rusted cars grazed in their yards. On their gates hung signs instructing the world to 'Keep Out'. They were not far from Eaglehawk but the Whipstick felt remote and isolated. Soon the houses disappeared and there was only bush. The car and caravan turned up a disused track and continued deep into the forest.

He removed the ropes, and Marnie felt relieved but she still agonized. *This creep is going to watch me pee.* But she was desperate, so she squatted on the ground in front of him.

"Do you mind not watching me go to the toilet?" asked Marnie, surprising herself with the strength of her voice and her courage to confront the man who was watching her.

She looked up and he was staring down at the wet patch.

Marnie knew she had to be a fast. It was getting on to dusk and it was now or never. She quickly straightened and tugged her undies up. Before he could react, she kicked him hard in the balls.

Then she ran.

Ahead of Marnie was a forest of spindly trees. They stood narrow and tall with a meagre canopy of dull eucalyptus leaves. The Whipstick's barren clay had neither the nutrients nor the moisture to allow these trees to develop a wider girth. They stood, constricted, like a mass of malnourished children waiting to be fed.

She could see deep into the forest. It was never-ending; around her was nothing but an endless vista of skinny trees.

Marnie despaired. *There's nowhere to hide.*

She kept running but it was hard going, little quartz stones rolled underfoot. Unnatural piles of gravel dotted the landscape. Marnie knew these were the earth taken from inside the mining shafts. She also knew most of the shafts were filled in but some were still open or had collapsed. With any stride she might fall into a deep abyss and would never get out.

"Wake up, wake up!" It was a voice with a strange accent. Marnie felt herself being lifted. "It's ok," said the voice reassuringly. "You had a bad fall and I'm taking you to my place."

"Who the hell are you?" she demanded.

"Jack Miller," the voice responded. It was dark and Marnie couldn't see him but she felt herself being carried through the forest. Her head throbbed, her body ached and she was exhausted.

In time they came to his place, which seemed to be just a camp erected on a gravelly indentation in the ground.

"Where am I?" Marnie said.

"This is Unfortunate Bolle's Mine," came the reply.

"Who's Unfortunate Bolle? I thought you said this was your place?"

The man was standing before her as she sat on the ground, nursing her sore head. He crouched down on his haunches, pushed back his wide-brimmed hat, and spoke slowly, reassuringly. "The name comes from a man called Jacob Bolle who had discovered gold here. That was many years ago. It's been my place for some time."

He stood up and busied himself with the campfire, stoking it with small sticks as it crackled in to life. "You take it easy," he told her. "In the morning, we'll walk out of the Whipstick to get help."

Marnie watched him for a moment, as his face was illuminated by the campfire. It was a kind face, she decided, and made a quick decision to confide in him.

"There was a weird guy," she said in a rush, her voice too loud in the quiet of the forest. "He grabbed me when I was coming home from school and threw me in his caravan," she explained. "He's evil, he tied me up in the caravan. I don't want to scare you but he'll probably come looking for me."

"Don't worry, I've been watching him," replied Jack. "He's left the Whipstick and taken his caravan with him."

"I remember running from him but I don't remember falling," said Marnie.

"You were lucky, I'm not often over that way. You fell into a mine. It was shallow but it took bit to get you out," explained Jack.

The small fire flickered more brightly and warm light danced across the blackness. Marnie could see her rescuer more clearly now. He was a boy about her age, clean shaven with dark hair and brown eyes.

Jack Miller wore a white collarless shirt and over it was a black waistcoat. His trousers were grey and his boots were worn but sturdy. They had buttons on them. Just like someone out of a fairy tale, Marnie thought.

"Why do you live here?" she enquired. "Are you homeless?"

"Good Lord, no!" answered Jack indignantly. "I have the entire Whipstick to call home."

When Jack Miller spoke, his accent was strange. He had a curious way of rolling the r sound in his words.

"Are you from overseas?" asked Marnie.

"Indeed I have travelled over the seas to get here," replied Jack Miller, smiling.

Marnie noticed the smile, but she was puzzled, and couldn't help interrogating him further, curious about how he lived out here in this harsh bush. "Do you have a job?" she asked.

"I am gainfully employed here at Unfortunate Bolle's mine," stated Jack, again with a small, patient smile.

"Oh great, you're a miner!'

He cheerfully agreed "Yes indeed, Miss. I first went down a mine when I was 10 years old."

"I was 11," replied Marnie. "All Bendigo kids in Year 6 have to visit The Central Deborah Gold Mine on a school excursion. It's part of learning about Bendigo's history."

Marnie remembered putting on a hard hat with a torch on the front. Then all the kids got into a lift which looked like a cage. They descended twenty stories below the famous Bendigo tourist attraction.

"There was a dining room down there and they served us pies and sausage rolls. I was so nervous I threw mine up," explained Marnie.

Jack laughed, "Pies and sausage rolls! Why the only thing you should eat in a mine is a pasty, Miss."

"You are so old-fashioned, Jack! The only person I know who eats pasties is my Mum," retorted Marnie. She realised with a small start that she had relaxed completely as she talked about mines and sausage rolls with this lanky lad. The campfire was cosy and she was almost comfortable as they chatted together in the dark.

Jack was silent for a moment. When he spoke, it was almost in a whisper. "You're lucky to have a Mother. My Ma died I was 12, she had the scarlet fever. Ma caught it from my two little brothers, they went to the Good Lord with her," confided Jack. "That just left my younger sister and me as well as our Pa. But he died when I was 14. It was the black lung which did him in."

"That must have been hard," said Marnie, her voice quiet too.

"It was especially hard on my little sister, that's why I decided to come here and make my fortune mining for gold so I could give my sister a good life, Miss."

"You don't have to keep calling me Miss, my name is Marnie."

Jack Miller stood and bowed, "It's an honour to make your acquaintance, Marnie."

She smiled, there was something about Jack's odd way of speaking that Marnie really liked. He was not like the boys at school. He didn't feel the need to show off. Certainly, he didn't have all that stuff – the iPhones, computer games or skateboards – that most boys showed off with, but that didn't appear to bother him. He seemed happy.

"Now would you like something to eat? I have some rabbit stew," offered Jack.

"Thanks, I'm starving," replied Marnie, even though she had never eaten rabbit stew before.

They shared a meal and Jack gave Marnie his coat for a blanket. As the fire died down, she fell asleep.

"This is as far as I go," said Jack.

"What do you mean?" asked Marnie.

"I don't like crowds," said Jack, hunching his shoulders.

They had walked all morning and found a picnic area where several families were enjoying an outing.

Marnie walked alone toward the people and let them know of her plight. Jack stayed behind in the bush.

Later, as the cuts on her legs were examined by a paramedic, Marnie could see Jack Miller watching from the scrub. She gave a secret knowing smile towards him.

It was the Year 11 history excursion day and the destination was Bendigo Library. Everyone was trying to sneak away to get a coffee over the road at Gillie's Pie Shop. Miss Munro planted herself beside the door and was doing a good job of preventing escapees.

A librarian had just given a talk on how to research local history. Marnie flipped open her laptop; there was one place she wanted to know more about.

In the three months since her ordeal in the Whipstick, Marnie had been seeing a counsellor and the police had arrested her kidnapper. They couldn't locate Jack.

Where was he? Was Jack Miller still out in the Whipstick working his mine?

Now she typed the words 'Unfortunate Bolle's mine', into the search engine. It was a programme designed to digitally search old copies of the local newspaper.

The first news story about Unfortunate Bolle's mine came up...

The Bendigo Advertiser

Thursday 14th June 1866. Page 3

Unfortunate incident at Unfortunate Bolle's Mine

Yesterday a young miner, 17 year old Jack Miller died when Unfortunate Bolle's mine collapsed. Jack Miller was trapped as the earth fell in on him. The mine shaft was totally destroyed and it was impossible to save him. The area was unstable so his body could not be recovered.

Jack Miller had arrived on the Whipstick diggings from Cornwell in August 1865. His only surviving relative is a sister, a chambermaid, in London.

Mr Jacob Bolle, owner of the mine, has written to his sister informing her of the sad news.

•

Girls In Our Town - an excerpt
Dianne Dempsey

PROLOGUE

IF you drive along the Calder Highway into the centre of Bendigo from the Melbourne side, you'll see the Gothic Sacred Heart Cathedral sitting supreme on a sloping lawn just behind the Yamaha bike shop. In some towns the value of your house is determined by whether you have a sea view, but in Bendigo, your status is based on whether or not you live by the cathedral.

Keep driving past the cathedral until you come to the Alexandra Fountain. Ignore the naked ladies and the horses, turn left and head in northerly direction for six kilometres until you get to the Borough. From there, keep driving until you find yourself in a vast forest known as the Whipstick.

Alluvial gold mining took place here in the 1850s and 1860s. The Whipstick is harsh, sandstone country with little water, covered by a dense mass of box-ironbark, mallee eucalyptus, wattle and dodder-laurel vines. In the early days of the gold rush, these parasitic vines were so pervasive they created a huge web in which diggers would often become lost and caught like flies, they suffered desperate, lonely deaths.

But before the diggers there were the Dja Dja Wurrung

people, and before them there were the spirits – ghost creatures – who were disturbed when the miners sunk their shafts and dug their tunnels. Later, huge crushing batteries pounded the gold-bearing quartz, night and day. The sound, they say, was terrible and the pounding made the earth tremble.

Ten years ago, when I was twenty, when my sister Brigid was thirteen and my mother, Clover, was thirty-seven, we lived in the forest in an old miner's cottage, and we too were lost.

I sometimes think with the benefit of hindsight and a dab of wisdom behind each ear I may have behaved differently; but truly, I don't regret what I eventually did, not one little bit.

CHAPTER ONE

IT was a Friday night in 1993 and I could hear the delicious pinging of rain on the tin roof of the cottage. The rain became so heavy that I had to strategically place ice cream containers on the floor under the places where the water got in.

I decided I would wait up for Clover and went to get some more wood for the fire. On my way out I tripped over Jackie Kennedy- Onassis who was asleep in the hallway. She shook her scraggy locks, snarled at me and shuffled off to find some other inconvenient spot. I remember noticing that she was going grey and my spirits lifted. She could die yet.

With kindling and rolled up newspaper I tenderly poked and prodded the fire until it roared into life again. I stayed crouched on my haunches for a time, just staring at the flames the way you do. I tidied up a bit, took the dirty dishes out to the kitchen and picked up Brigid's dirty socks and threw them into the bin - that'd teach her. Finally I wiped up the trails of Clover's incense ash, which curled over all the surfaces like little grey worms.

I wanted to talk to Clover about a problem I had. It shouldn't be so hard to pin your mother down but Clover had me when she was seventeen, reluctantly. Abortions were hard to come by back then. I know this because I heard her tell her friends so, many times, usually when in the grip of the juice or gurgling away at a bong. I think they all thought I was asleep when they went on like that but I wasn't, I was just in the next room listening. I was always listening.

Because Clover was such a shit of a parent I often looked after my little sister Brigid as well doing things like keeping the home fires burning. But every now and then I jacked up. I tried to coach Clover into playing grown-ups – pretend she loved me the way a proper mother should. I might have been twenty, but I still needed someone to talk to.

I decided I'd make her some supper this night. There was a matter I wanted to talk to her about. Just a small matter of my heart. I wandered back out into the freezing kitchen to see what was in the fridge. The kitchen was originally the back veranda of the cottage and there was a nasty step down to it from the rest of the house. People sometimes forgot about this step especially at parties for some reason and ended up on the floor – kaboom.

Lethal drafts crept in under the kitchen door. The gas stove was under the chimney piece and you had to practically stick your head up the chimney in order to stir the pots. There were horrible, sooty stringy cobwebs that hung down from inside the chimney that sometimes dropped into your pan of bacon and eggs. A single sink was squeezed into a corner next to the fridge and the floor was covered in crappy lino and rugs over which we kept tripping. The only room worse than the kitchen was the mouldy bathroom that led off it.

The living room was stuffed with a sagging couch, an assortment of chairs, the television and piles of books, which would spontaneously collapse when the weight of the ashtrays and plates became too much.

We tried to brighten things up in our own way. Clover hung up her paintings of dopey angels who looked like they were on a permanent all-time high. Periodically Brigid and I would pick wattle or tiny orchids. We would put them in vases and jars, place them around the cottage and then watch while they slowly died.

It was when I was prodding an ancient sausage in the fridge that I heard a knock on the kitchen door. I jumped. I went to open it and then stopped. I could hear my pulse beating in my ears. Jackie O barked furiously.

"Who's there?" I whispered. I was surprised at how scared I sounded. There was no answer except for another round of knocking. If people came out here they usually drove and I'd heard no engine rumbling, nor car doors slamming. I snipped the lock on the door and stepped back from it like it was on fire.

I felt a tug on my jumper and looked around to see Brigid staring at me, wide-eyed. She still had her tooth brush in her hand and the white foam around her mouth made me think she had rabies, which wouldn't have surprised me in the least, such was the generally fetid state of her health. We were all of us – Jackie O, Brigid and myself – of a single thought. Someone was knocking on the door and it wasn't the Avon lady.

Brigid started to hop from foot to foot. "Dad," she called out, "Dad! There's someone at the door." The point being of course that we didn't have a dad, well, there were a couple out there somewhere but none in the house. For good measure she called out, "Dad, call the police." Then we heard something worse than knocking – silence.

I raced to the front door and made sure it was locked. Brigid grabbed the phone and looked at me blankly. "Triple O," I hissed at her.

I picked up the poker by the fire and stared wildly around the room, the bastard was out there somewhere. I could hear Brigid whispering down the phone and snatched it off her.

"Someone's trying to break into our house," I breathlessly told them. When the voice at the other end asked me to check the number and try again my heart sank. How did she do it? And she did it so often, manage to make a bad situation absolutely ten times worse.

The knocking was on the front door now. I raced to it and turned on the outside light. I called out again. "Who's there?" I waited. I couldn't bear standing there with those cowards, Jackie O and Brigid, staring at me any longer. I rushed to the door and flung it open. The garden was dark and wet and leaping with shadows. "I know you're there!" I yelled.

Jackie O dashed outside, chased her tail a couple of times and then darted back in again. One half of her was a Jack Russell, fearless and proud and the other half was a sneaky, shoe- chewing, flatulent fraud. I grabbed a shovel and passed Brigid a broom. "Come on Bridge," I said, "back-to-back."

Walking back-to-back is quite hard. "Forwards Bridge," I whispered. "No, I mean forwards this way. My way, you idiot." We managed to walk up and down the veranda and then I guided us down the steps and to garden path where the light was much poorer.

"Dad," Brigid called out. "Dad, have you finished in the toilet yet?"

"Listen," I hissed.

We heard gums leaves shaking in the wind and felt the heavy drops of rain on our faces. I registered the pungent smell of our big peppercorn tree which stood guard over the house and illogically, I felt comforted. I peered into the darkness and the forest beyond.

I thought I saw a light flickering and fading and weaving its way through the dense darkness of trees and bush. There was something out there, I was sure. But there always was.

www.ingramcontent.com/pod-product-compliance
Lightning Source LLC
Chambersburg PA
CBHW061126100726
47911CB00013B/695